W9-BUZ-789

Disney

TSUM TSUM

book of haiku

SUSTAINABLE FORESTRY INITIATIVE

Certified Sourcing
www.sfiprogram.org
SFI-00993

This Label Applies to Text Stock Only

Special thanks to the talented Disney haiku writers—you know who you are.

Copyright © 2015 Disney Enterprises, Inc. All rights reserved.
Pixar characters and artwork Copyright © Disney and Pixar.
Based on the "Winnie the Pooh" works by A.A. Milne and E.H. Shepard.
Published by Disney Press, an imprint of Disney Book Group. No part of this book may be
reproduced or transmitted in any form or by any means, electronic or mechanical,
including photocopying, recording, or by any information
storage and retrieval system, without written permission from the publisher.
For information address Disney Press, 1101 Flower Street, Glendale, California 91201.

First Hardcover Edition, October 2015   10 9 8 7 6 5 4 3 2 1

ISBN: 978-1-4847-2925-0
FAC-038091-15233
Library of Congress Control Number: 2014955965
Printed in the United States of America
For more Disney Press fun, visit www.disneybooks.com

Designed by Megan Rickards Youngquist

Disney

"TSUM TSUM"

book of
haiku

Disney PRESS
Los Angeles • New York

haiku

is a form of Japanese poetry that is recognized and enjoyed around the world.

In haiku, a poem must adhere to the following structure:
The poem must consist of **17 syllables.**
The syllables are arranged in **three lines of 5-7-5.**

Haiku poems are celebrated for their simple and expressive nature—as you will discover through our lively and colorful Tsum Tsum characters!

5   7   5

Nice little fellow,

And a bit **mischief**

ievOus, too;

Leader of the band.

Dressing for success
Or dressing just for yourself,

All's good with a bow.

Best friend of Mickey,

Bedeviled by those chipmunks,

Time to take a nap.

Woody set on top
And **Bullseye** stacked below him.
Yee-haw! Off we go!

Little alien,
Hanging upside down, watching

As Tsum Tsum

Buzz flies.

She can be **fiesty**

And short with Donald sometimes,
But can you blame her?

Tsum Tsum all alone,

Searching for somewhere to stack:

626, or **Stitch.**

In a plush forest,
Tsum Tsum **Pooh and Piglet** stand
Stacked close, **side by side**.

Ladies don't start fights

But they sure can finish them,

And **I'm a Lady**.

Jessie at the **top**,
Buzz sits tight in the **middle**,
Woody down **below**.

If I made the rules,
No one would be able to

Make me stop

bouncing.

Goofy stacked on top
Of **Pluto, Mickey, Donald**;
But under the girls.

When he first saw her,
Those ears, that smile, he just knew
It was meant to be.

Yo  -oh
-dee

-oh!

-ee

Woody's Round-up's favorite Yodeling cowgirl!

His friends behind him,
Pooh Bear mumbles, "Oh, bother!"
What's the trouble now?

Adorable Hamm,
On a mound of other toys,
King Little Piggy.

He has a temper,

But just remember his heart

Is in the right place.

Down the rabbit hole,

Eat me, drink me; which way's up?

Must be **Wonderland**!

Snow White, the fairest

In all of the land and sea,

Don't eat the **apple**!

How I wish there were

Some honey in my tummy!

Sending pleas to beeeeeeeeeee

eees.

It's so **magical**

To **come alive** and **run 'round**

When we are **alone**.

Follow the rabbit.
I'm late, I'm late! Hurry now,
Wonderland awaits!

Flap your ears

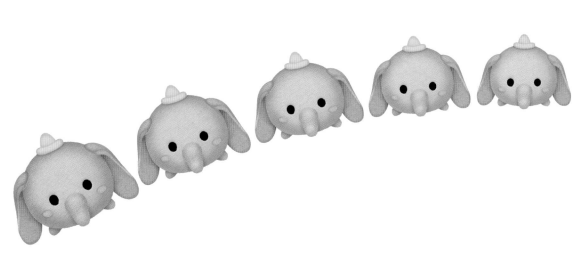

and soar

Like a weightless baby bird

To endless applause.

Wide grin, shining smile,
It lingers once he is gone,
Crescent moon of teeth.

Sensational Six:
Immortal cartoon faces.

Disney's dreams